HUMBLE PIE

For Wilfriede and Matt, my parents, and Mary, my grandmother. With love.
—J. D.
For Puss, with a certain amount of affection.
—S. G.

HUMBLE PIE

STORY BY
JENNIFER DONNELLY

PICTURES BY
STEPHEN GAMMELL

A RICHARD JACKSON BOOK
Atheneum Books for Young Readers

New York London Toronto Sydney Singapore

Once upon a time, and a long time ago it was, there lived a very bad boy named Theo.

He thought of nobody besides himself. He never helped his father with the chores, or shared his toys, or gave a penny to a poor beggar. He never gave a bite of sausage to the dog or a lick of milk to the cat.

No one knew why Theo was so awful, but some had theories. His uncle said he ate too much pepper. The village apothecary said he had a small troll living inside him. Just below his liver. Only Theo's grandmother knew the truth: The boy was spoiled rotten! His parents made too much of him. His mother wove him tunics of the softest flax, and his father made him a leather pouch for his pennies. He had a plump feather bed and a warm coverlet. He had a crimson cap and a beautiful hobbyhorse.

You would think that Theo might appreciate all that his parents had worked so hard to give him. Not a bit. The more he got, the more he wanted. He became demanding and arrogant. Selfish. Thoughtless. Inconsiderate. Grabby. Unkind. Bumptious, rude, and lazy. Obnoxious. Obstreperous. High-handed. And mouthy.

One day, when the bread wouldn't rise and the cat had kittens in the sewing basket and Meg the servant girl burned the stew and Theo's mother's patience was gone, Theo came in and grabbed a basket of strawberries she had just picked.

"Theo, don't eat those! They're for Baby Tom's birthday cake," she scolded, tugging on the basket.

"But I want them!" he said, tugging back. He pulled so hard, the basket split and the berries went flying. They splattered on the floor like big red raindrops.

Theo knew he was in trouble. He ran out of the kitchen before his mother could catch him and through the woods to his grandmother's house. He found her in her yard making a pie. She was rolling out the top crust, making it bigger with every push of her rolling pin. Bigger than a nine-inch pie, bigger than a ten-inch pie. Bigger than a tablecloth. Bigger than a bedsheet. So big, in fact, that when she was done, she had to hang it over her clothesline.

"What kind of pie *is* that, Grandmother?" Theo asked.

The old woman smiled a wise smile. "Humble pie, child," she said.

"I want some!"

"You shall have plenty," she said, filling the pie with buckets of fruit. As she worked, she sang a funny little song:

FLOUR, BUTTER, SALT SAY I,
BERRIES, CHERRIES, PILE THEM HIGH,
HUSH NOW, MOTHER, DON'T YOU SIGH,
LET THE BOY EAT HUMBLE PIE.

Greedy Theo leaned against the pie and snatched a cherry. He leaned over farther and reached for a plum. As he was about to grab it, he lost his balance and toppled forward. Quick as a wink, his grandmother flipped the top crust over him and crimped the edges. Theo was sealed in the pie!

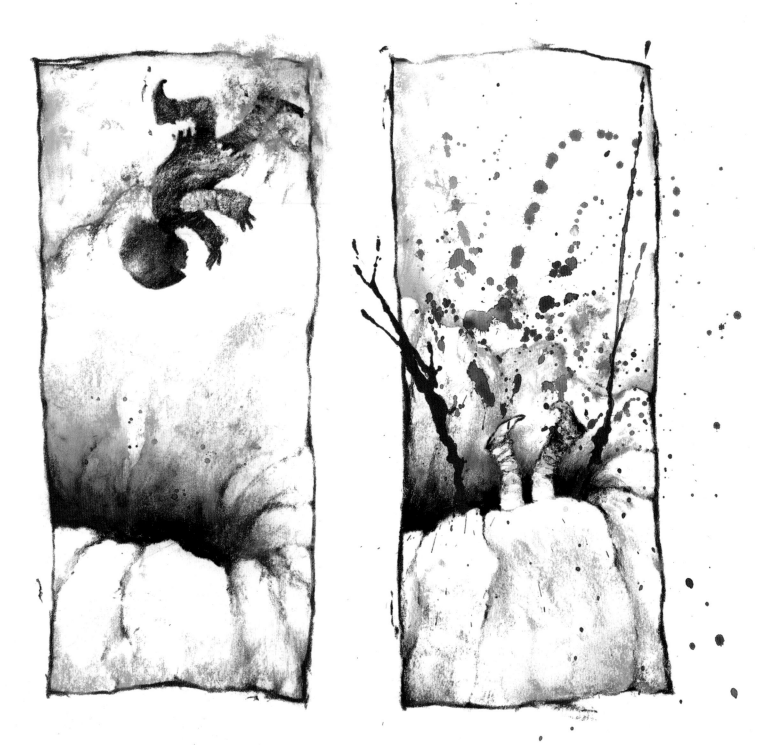

"HELLLLP!!" he shouted. "Grandmother, get me out!"

"Only you can do that, child," she said. And then she went inside, still singing her pie song:

FLOUR, BUTTER, SALT SAY I,
PLUMS AND PEACHES,
PILE THEM HIGH,
THE CHILD WILL SHOUT,
THE CHILD WILL CRY,
UNTIL he's TASTED HUMBLE PIE.

Furious, Theo launched into the biggest temper tantrum you have ever seen. He kicked and screamed. He pummeled the top crust. He stamped on the bottom crust. He threw himself from side to side and rocked the pie so hard that it tipped upright onto its edge. He found he could roll forward this way and that he could see out of the steam holes.

"I know what to do," he said. "I'll roll home. Mama will cut me out with her sewing scissors."

On the way to his house, he passed some of his schoolmates playing King of the Hill. "Maud, Alfred, Eleanor, Baldrick!" he shouted. "It's me, Theo!"

"Theo?" Alfred said, prodding the pie with his wooden sword. "Is that really you?"

"Yes! Help! Get me out!"

But no one did.

Maud said: "He boasts and brags and wants his own way."

Alfred said: "He never takes turns and he never shares."

Eleanor said: "He tattles and tells and always makes trouble."

Baldrick said nothing. He just gave the pie a push. The others joined in and got it rolling. The pie rolled fast. Whenever it hit a pothole, it flew high into the air and landed with a bang. Theo was bounced and trounced and jounced.

By the time he got home, he was dizzy. He had a lump on his head and a scrape on his knee. He couldn't wait to get out of the pie. His family was sure to be worried about him. They were certain to miss him. Why, they probably missed him so much, they were crying their eyes out.

But when he rolled up to the kitchen window, he saw that they weren't crying. They were laughing. Meg was singing, and Fred the stable boy was playing the mandolin. His grandmother was serving cake and cider. His parents were dancing. The dog and cat were dancing, too. They were all celebrating Baby Tom's birthday.

Bewildered, Theo slumped down inside the pie, knocking it against the house. His father heard the noise. Thinking it was an animal, he sent the dog to chase it away. The cat went, too. Theo saw them. "Go dog! Go cat!" he shouted. "Get my mother and father!" But the dog and cat didn't go anywhere. They thought about all the kicks and slaps they'd received from Theo. And all the times he'd refused to give them a bite of his supper. Then they rolled the pie to the edge of a hill behind the house and let it go. Down the hill and through the woods it went. Wham! Bang! Crash!

Theo howled and yowled and thumped and bumped over rocks and ruts and branches. By the time the pie came to a stop, he had another lump on his head and an ugly bruise on his elbow. Where am I? he wondered, wincing as he rubbed his sore spots. He looked out and saw a village. Maybe somebody there can get me out, he thought.

INTRODUCTION

When I was a boy, adults I knew went to the trouble of helping me find a few heroes. At first, the ones I admired most were not people I knew personally, but figures who nonetheless possessed qualities of human excellence worth striving for: baseball and football players who persevered on and off the field, famous explorers from the pages of history who dared to face the unknown, cowboys from Hollywood Westerns who rode hard and stood up for what deserved to be loved and protected. As I grew older, I learned that heroes could be found closer to home, too—neighbors, friends, and members of my own family. In all of them, there was a certain nobility, a largeness of soul, a hitching up of one's own purposes to higher purposes—to something that demanded endurance or sacrifice or courage or compassion.

Looking back, I see how lucky I was that so many of my teachers thought it was worth their time to help me pick the right kind of heroes. As every parent knows, children imitate what they see and hear. They naturally look for examples to follow. Today's popular culture offers plenty. Countless "stars" and "superstars" are put on pedestals for children to idolize and mimic. The problem is that most are celebrities, not heroes (it has been said that the difference between the two is that while the hero is known for worthy actions, the celebrity is known for being well known). And often, especially in our times, the behaviors for which many celebrities are famous are not worthy of imitation. But little children don't know that. They can't foresee that some pedestals, in time, turn out to be shaky and come crashing down. So it makes a big difference whether or not adults make efforts to point out what actions merit honor and which individuals deserve to be admired.

This book is meant to aid parents in such efforts. Its heroes give young people targets to aim for and examples to follow. Their tales come to life in Michael Hague's charming, magical paintings, which speak to the hearts

and imaginations of children. The combination of a few good stories, Michael's illustrations, and a parent's voice reading aloud is a great way to lift children's thoughts toward what is noble and fine.

Some of these heroes are doers of ancient, famous deeds ("mighty men which were of old, men of renown," as the book of Genesis has it)—shining victors, knights in armor, adventurers on the high seas. Their stories often unfold in far-off places—dusty plains, stormy seas, dungeons dark, castles high. Theirs are tales of epic drama—battles against overwhelming odds, daring rescues, struggles to the death, triumphs of good over evil.

But in truth, most heroes are not men and women of great renown. They live close by and, more often than not, perform deeds noticed by only a few. You'll find those kinds of heroes here, too. They come from every walk of life—boys and girls, mothers and fathers, men and women of God, teachers, a neighbor lending a helping hand, the cop around the corner. They win our admiration by committing the sort of acts every one of us might be called upon to perform—by offering some unseen gesture of compassion, by taking a quiet stand for what is right, by managing to hang on just one minute longer, or perhaps by persevering through a lifetime of struggle and toil.

Some of the heroes in this book are real people. They have lived and breathed, just as you and I. Others tread only the worlds of our imaginations. But factual or fictional, they all put a face on and give a meaning to heroism. They give us a chance to say to children, "Look, there is a person who has done something worth imitating."

It is important to say that to children, because believing in the heroic can help make each and every one of us a little bit better, day in and day out. If our children are to reach for the best, they need to have a picture of the best.

I hope this book helps boys and girls to believe in heroes. I hope it inspires parents and children to look around them and together pick out a few heroes of their own.

Heroes

～ WILLIAM CANTON

Our favorite heroes live forever in their stories and in our
memories, cheering us forward in our own brave fights.

For you who love heroic things
In summer dream or winter tale,
I tell of warriors, saints, and kings,
In scarlet, sackcloth, glittering mail,
And helmets peaked with iron wings.

They beat down Wrong; they strove for Right.
In ringing fields, on grappled ships,
Singing, they flung into the fight.
They fell with triumph on their lips,
And in their eyes a glorious light.

That light still gleams. From far away
Their brave song greets us like a cheer.
We fight the same great fight as they,
Right against Wrong; we, now and here;
They, in their fashion, yesterday.

9

Opportunity

EDWARD ROWLAND SILL

It's not the sword you use that makes you a hero. It's how you use the sword.

This I beheld, or dreamed it in a dream:
There spread a cloud of dust along a plain;
And underneath the cloud, or in it, raged
A furious battle, and men yelled, and swords
Shocked upon swords and shields. A prince's banner
Wavered, then staggered backward, hemmed by foes.
A craven hung along the battle's edge,
And thought: "Had I a sword of keener steel—
That blue blade that the king's son bears—but this
Blunt thing—!" he snapt and flung it from his hand,
And lowering crept away and left the field.
Then came the king's son, wounded, sore bestead,
And weaponless, and saw the broken sword,
Hilt buried in the dry and trodden sand,
And ran and snatched it, and with battle shout
Lifted afresh, he hewed his enemy down,
And saved a great cause that heroic day.

About Angels

— ADAPTED FROM LAURA E. RICHARDS

Here is a story about a guardian angel who is always close at hand, the kind who watches over you from the moment you come into the world.

"Mother," said the child, "are there really angels?"

"The Bible says so," said the mother.

"Yes," said the child. "I have seen the picture. But did you ever see one, Mother?"

"I think I have," said the mother, "but she was not dressed like the picture."

"I am going to find one!" said the child. "I am going to run along the road, miles and miles and miles, until I find an angel."

"That is a good plan!" said the mother. "And I will go with you, for you are too little to run far alone."

"I am not little anymore!" said the child. "I can tie my own shoes. I am big."

"So you are!" said the mother. "I forgot. But it is a fine day, and I should like the walk."

"But you walk so slowly, with your hurt foot."

"I can walk faster than you think!" said the mother.

11

So they started, the child leaping and running, and the mother stepping out so bravely with her injured foot that the child soon forgot about it.

The child danced ahead, and soon he saw a long, silver car coming toward him. In the back sat a splendidly dressed lady. As she moved in her seat, she flashed with jewels and gold, and her eyes were brighter than her diamonds.

The car rolled to a halt at a stop sign.

"Are you an angel?" asked the child, running up beside it.

The lady made no reply, but stared coldly at the child. Then she spoke a word to her driver, and the engine roared. The car sped away in a cloud of dust and fumes, and disappeared.

The dust filled the child's eyes and mouth, and made him choke and sneeze. He gasped for breath and rubbed his eyes, but presently his mother came up and wiped away the dust with the corner of her dress.

"That was not an angel!" said the child.

"No, indeed!" said the mother. "Nothing like one!"

The child danced on again, leaping and running from side to side of the road, and the mother followed as best she could.

By and by the child met a most beautiful young woman, clad in a white dress. Her eyes were like blue stars, and the blushes came and went in her face like roses looking through snow.

"I am sure you must be an angel!" cried the child.

The young woman blushed more sweetly than before. "You dear little child!" she cried. "Someone else said that only last evening. Do I really look like an angel?"

"You *are* an angel!" said the child.

The young woman took him up in her arms, and kissed him, and held him tenderly. "You are the dearest little thing I ever saw!" she said. "Tell me what makes you think so!" But suddenly her face changed.

"Oh!" she cried. "There he is, coming to meet me! And you have soiled my white dress with your dusty shoes, and messed up my beautiful hair. Run away, child, and go home to your mother!"

She set the child down, not unkindly, but so hastily that he stumbled and fell. But she did not see that, for she was hastening to meet her boyfriend, who was coming along the road. (Now if the young woman had only known, he thought her twice as lovely with the child in her arms, but she did not know.)

The child lay in the dusty road and sobbed, till his mother came along, picked him up, and wiped away the tears.

"I don't believe that was an angel, after all," he said.

"No!" said the mother. "But she may be one someday. She is young yet."

"I am tired!" said the child. "Will you carry me home, Mother?"

"Why, yes!" said the mother. "That is what I came for."

The child put his arms around his mother's neck, and she held him tight and trudged along the road, singing the song he liked best. Suddenly he looked up into her face.

"Mother," he said, "I don't suppose *you* could be an angel, could you?"

"Oh, my little one!" said the mother. "I am just your mother who loves you." And she went on singing, and stepped out so happily on her injured foot that she forgot her pain and felt only joy with her young son.

Sail On! Sail On!

~ JOAQUIN MILLER

*Sometimes being a hero means having the courage and determination to say,
"Forward!" while the crowd all around you cries, "Turn back!"*

Behind him lay the gray Azores,
Behind the gates of Hercules;
Before him not the ghost of shores,
Before him only shoreless seas.
The good mate said: "Now must we pray,
For lo! the very stars are gone;
Speak, Admiral, what shall I say?"
"Why say, sail on! and on!"

"My men grow mut'nous day by day;
My men grow ghastly wan and weak."
The stout mate thought of home; a spray
Of salt wave wash'd his swarthy cheek.
"What shall I say, brave Admiral,
If we sight naught but seas at dawn?"
"Why, you shall say, at break of day:
'Sail on! sail on! and on!'"

They sailed and sailed, as winds might blow,
Until at last the blanch'd mate said:
"Why, now, not even God would know
Should I and all my men fall dead.
These very winds forget their way,
For God from these dread seas is gone.
Now speak, brave Admiral, and say—"
He said: "Sail on! and on!"

They sailed, they sailed, then spoke his mate:
"This mad sea shows his teeth tonight,
He curls his lip, he lies in wait,
With lifted teeth as if to bite!
Brave Admiral, say but one word;
What shall we do when hope is gone?"
The words leaped as a leaping sword:
"Sail on! sail on! and on!"

Then, pale and worn, he kept his deck,
And thro' the darkness peered that night.
Ah, darkest night! and then a speck—
A light! a light! a light! a light!
It grew—a star-lit flag unfurled!
It grew to be Time's burst of dawn;
He gained a world! he gave that world
Its watchword: "On! and on!"

"I'll try now," offered the Vulture. "Maybe this journey calls for someone with wings."

So the Vulture flew east, and finally he came to the sun. He dived and snatched a piece of it in his claws.

"Possum tried to carry the sun with his tail and dropped it," he told himself. "I'll try carrying it on my head."

Vulture set the piece of sun on his head and turned for home, but the sun was so hot that before long it had burned away all the feathers on his crown. He grew dizzy and lost his way, and began wandering around and around until the piece of sun tumbled to the ground. That is why today a vulture's head is bald, and you'll still see him drifting in circles high overhead.

"Now we're truly finished," the animals cried when Vulture returned in darkness. "Possum and Vulture tried as best they could, but it wasn't enough."

"Maybe we need to try one more time," a tiny voice rose from the weeds. "I'll go this time."

"Who is that?" the animals asked. "Who said that?"

"It's me, Old Lady Spider. I know I'm small and slow, but perhaps I'm the one who can make it."

Before she started, she gathered a bit of wet clay, and with her eight tiny hands she made a little pot.

"Possum and Vulture had nothing to carry the sun in," she said. "I'll put it in this pot."

Then she spun a thread and fastened the end to a rock.

"The sun's bright light hurt Possum's eyes, and its heat made Vulture so dizzy he lost his way," she said. "But I'll follow this thread home."

So she set out, traveling east, spinning her thread behind her as she walked. When she reached the sun, she pinched off a small piece and put it in her clay pot. It was still so bright she could hardly see, but she turned and followed her thread home.

She came walking out of the east all aglow, looking like the sun itself. And even today, when Old Lady Spider spins her web, it looks like the rays of the rising sun.

She reached home at last. All the animals could see for the first time. They saw how tiny and old Spider was, and they wondered that she could make the journey alone. Then they saw how she had carried the sun in the little pot, and that was when the world learned to make pots out of clay and set them in the sun to dry.

But Old Lady Spider had had enough of being so close to the sun. That is why, today, she spins her web in the early morning hours, before the sun is too high and hot.

The Star Jewels

⁓ ADAPTED FROM THE BROTHERS GRIMM

This beautiful little story echoes the words we find in the Gospel of Matthew: "I was hungry and you gave me food. . . . I was naked and you clothed me."

A little girl once lived all alone with her old grandmother on the borders of a forest. They were so poor that they were scarcely able to buy food to eat or clothes to cover them.

"Never mind, Granny," the little girl would say. "Someday I will be big enough to work, and then I will earn so much that I will be able to buy everything that we need, and to give something to other poor folk as well."

One day the child went off into the forest to gather sticks. These she hoped to sell for a few pennies in the town over beyond the hill. She was to be gone all day, so she took with her into the forest a bit of bread, which was all they had left to eat.

It was winter, and the air was bitterly cold. The child wrapped her little shawl about her and ran on as fast as she could. She was hungry, but she intended to save her crust until after the sticks were gathered.

Just as she reached the edge of the forest she met a boy even smaller than herself, and he was crying bitterly.

The little girl had a tender heart. She stopped and asked the child why he was weeping.

"I am weeping," he answered, "because I am hungry."

"Have you had nothing to eat today?" she asked.

"I have had nothing, and I am starving, for I do not know where to go for food."

The little girl sighed. "You are probably hungrier than I am," she said, and she took the crust from her pocket and gave it to the boy. Then she again hurried on.

A little farther on, she met another child, who was even more miserable looking than the first, for this child seemed almost frozen with cold. Her clothing hung about her in rags, and her skin looked blue through the holes.

"Ah," cried she, "if I had but a warm little dress like yours! Help me, I pray you, or I will certainly die of cold."

The good little girl was filled with pity. "I have both a dress and a shawl," she thought. "I will give one of them to this poor child."

She took off her dress and gave it to the child, and then wrapped the shawl closely about her shoulders. In spite of the shawl she felt very cold. Still, she was near the place where the sticks were to be found, and as soon as she had gathered them, she would run home again.

She hastened on, but when she reached the place where the sticks were, she saw an old woman already there, gathering up the fallen wood. The old woman was so bent and poor and miserable looking that the little girl's heart ached for her.

"Oh, oh!" groaned the old woman. "How my poor bones do ache. If I had but a shawl to wrap about my shoulders I would not suffer so."

The child thought of her own grandmother and of how she sometimes suffered, and she took pity on the old woman.

"Here," said she. "Take my shawl," and slipping it from her shoulders, she gave it to the old woman.

And now she stood there in the forest with her arms and shoulders bare, and with nothing on her but her little shift. The sharp wind blew about her, but she was not cold. She had eaten nothing, but she was not hungry. She was fed and warmed by her own kindness.

She gathered her sticks and started home again. It was growing dark and the stars shone through the bare branches of the trees. Suddenly an old man stood beside her. "Give me your sticks," said he, "for my hearth is cold, and I am too old to gather wood for myself."

The little girl sighed. If she gave him the sticks she would have to stop to gather more. Still, she would not refuse him. "Take them," she said, "in heaven's name."

No sooner had she said this than she saw it was not an old man who stood before her, but a shining angel.

"You have fed the hungry," said the angel. "You have clothed the naked, and you have given help to those who asked it. You shall not go unrewarded. See!"

At once a light shone around the child, and it seemed to her that all the stars of heaven were falling through the bare branches of the trees. But these stars were diamonds and rubies and other precious stones. They lay thick upon the ground. "Gather them together," said the angel, "for they are yours."

Wondering, the child gathered them together—all that she could carry in the skirt of her little shift.

When she looked about her again, the angel was gone, and the child hastened home with her treasure. It was enough to make her and her old grandmother rich. From then on they lacked for nothing. They were able not only to have all they wished for, but to give to many who were poor. So they were not only rich, but beloved by all who knew them.

Mother Teresa

Great heroes aren't only in stories of old and history books. They live and breathe and walk among us. Here is a modern-day heroine who has devoted her life to helping the needy all over the world.

In faraway India, in a city called Calcutta, there lives a woman named Mother Teresa. She is a small woman. Her back is bent with age. Her hands are rough from a lifetime of toil. Her face is wrinkled, but her eyes are steady and bright.

Mother Teresa is a nun, a woman of God. She lives in a large house with other women, who call one another "Sister," for they are like a family. They all have given their lives to God and try to do His work.

If you could go visit Mother Teresa and spend a day with her, what would you see?

She rises from bed very early in the morning, long before the sun rises. She says her prayers, eats her breakfast, and does her chores with the sisters. Then she leaves her house and goes into the streets.

Follow her, and you will see her walk into parts of the city where the buildings are dirty, the streets are full of trash, and the people wear sad, tired looks on their faces. She sees a child, perhaps no older than you, sitting against the wall. His clothes are ragged and his face is covered with dirt. He does not have a home. He does not know where his parents are.

Mother Teresa stops. She takes him by the hand. She wipes the dirt off his face and the tears from his eyes. She leads him to a place where the sisters will give him a bath and new clothes. Then they will try to find a family who will love him and take him into their home.

Then one morning Helen and Annie were walking outside when they passed an old well. Annie took Helen's hand and held it under the spout while she pumped. As the cold water rushed forth, Annie spelled W-A-T-E-R.

Helen stood still. In one hand she felt the cool, gushing water. In the other hand she felt Annie's fingers, making the signs over and over again. Suddenly a thrill of hope and joy filled her little heart. She understood that W-A-T-E-R meant the wonderful, cool something that was flowing over her hand. She understood at last what Annie had been trying to show her for days and weeks. She saw now that everything had a name, and that she could use her fingers to spell out each name!

Helen ran laughing and crying back to the house, pulling Annie along with her. She touched everything she could lay her hands on, asking for their names—*chair, table, door, mother, father, baby,* and many more. There were so many wonderful words to learn! But none was more wonderful than the word Helen learned when she touched Annie to ask her name, and Annie spelled T-E-A-C-H-E-R.

Helen Keller never stopped learning. She learned to read with her fingers, and how to write, and even how to speak. She went to school and to college, and Annie went with her to help her learn. Helen and Annie became friends for life.

Helen Keller grew up to be a great woman. She devoted her life to helping people who could not see or hear. She worked hard, and wrote books, and traveled across the seas. Everywhere she went, she brought people courage and hope. Presidents and kings greeted her, and the whole world grew to love her. A childhood that had begun in darkness and loneliness turned into a life full of much light and joy.

"And the most important day in my life," Helen said, "was the day my teacher came to me."

Father Flanagan

Here is the real-life story of a man who believed every boy needs a hero called father.

If you ever go to the state of Nebraska, you will find a very special town of children. The young citizens of this wonderful little village vote to elect their own mayor and council members, who might be boys or girls just a few years older than you. They hold their own court whenever someone breaks the rules. Like any city, their town has its own post office and fire station. It has schools, ball fields, movie theaters, and even its own town band.

This is the story of Father Flanagan, the man who founded such a marvelous place. He was born in Ireland, but when he was a young man he came to the United States to be a priest. His church was in Omaha, Nebraska, where our story begins.

Omaha had a problem—boys! Unlike most children, these boys had no mothers and fathers to look after them. Many of them had no homes, and no one to love them and show them right from wrong. And so, some of them got into trouble. They broke store windows, stole fruit from the grocer, and fought in the street.

When Father Flanagan saw their hungry faces and ragged clothes, it broke his heart.

"Those boys should be arrested," said the grocer. "They need to be taken away."

Father Flanagan shook his head. "What they need is a home," he said. "They need someone to love them."

"But who would take them in?" asked the grocer.

"Maybe I will," said Father Flanagan.

And he did. He borrowed a few dollars to rent an old house, and trudged from door to door, asking for used furniture, plates, cups, spoons, blankets, rugs, and anything else his neighbors would give away. When he told people what he was doing, they thought he was crazy. But they also saw a kind, good man and gave him what they could.

He started with just five boys and gave them a place to eat, sleep, play, and pray. He gave them a home where they could feel safe and warm.

This was just what they needed. Before long they were laughing, learning, and growing up strong. When people saw what Father Flanagan was doing, they brought him more homeless and orphan boys. Before long he had outgrown his house and had to find a bigger one. But more and more boys came, and soon they had outgrown the new house too.

"These boys need a place all to themselves," thought Father Flanagan, "where they can run and play in fresh air, go to school and church, and grow up to be fine young men. They need a town of their own."

And that is just what Father Flanagan gave them. Outside of Omaha he found a farm for sale. He had no money to buy the land, but that did not stop him. Once again he went to friends and neighbors for help. When they heard what he had in mind, they were puzzled. A town for boys nobody wanted? Whoever heard of such a thing? But they knew that when Father Flanagan got an idea, he would never give up. So they pitched in to help him buy the farm and build his town.

Before too long, the streets and sidewalks of Boys Town covered the fields. Father Flanagan and his friends built houses and shops. They built a church and a post office. They built a big dining room where all the boys could eat and a pool where they could swim. And from all over the country, boys without mothers or fathers to take care of them came to Boys Town, where Father Flanagan gave them a home.

One day a boy who could not walk came to Boys Town. He was a tiny fellow, so Father Flanagan asked one of the bigger boys to carry him to his room. The big boy hoisted the newcomer onto his back.

"He's not too heavy, is he?" Father Flanagan asked.

"He ain't heavy, Father. He's my brother!" The older boy smiled.

And that was the best thing of all about Father Flanagan's Boys Town. The boys who came there found a family of hundreds of brothers who took care of each other, and a father who loved them all.

Boys Town is still there today, and if you ever go to Nebraska, you can visit it and see it for yourself. The wonderful town is still full of boys—and girls now, too—who have no parents to take care of them. You can see them laughing, playing, and studying their books, and growing up to be strong, good people. And when you see the smiles on their faces, you can remember the story of the father who built the town so many children have called home.

The Hero of Indian Cliff

~ ADAPTED FROM C. H. CLAUDY

This is a story about true brotherhood, about putting yourself on the line for someone you love.

High above a valley floor, in the giant Rocky Mountains of Colorado, two brothers climbed a steep mountainside. Higher and higher they hiked, until it seemed they would reach the sky itself.

The older brother went first. He carried a knapsack of food, a canteen full of cold water, and a long coil of rope. Sometimes, when the trail grew very steep, he would tie the rope around a tree and throw the other end to his brother, to make it easier for him to follow.

"Get a good grip on the rope, Nando," he would call. "And watch where you plant your feet."

For a whole year, Nando had been waiting for this hike. Today he was nine years old. For a birthday present, his brother, Manuel, was finally showing him the way to a secret lookout—Indian Cliff!

Manuel was almost twelve, and he had been coming to Indian Cliff for two years now. He was sure of the path and could climb as quickly as a mountain goat. But today he went slowly, to help Nando along.

Sometimes Nando would try to climb too fast, and then he would lose his breath.

"Take your time, Nando," Manuel would say. "We'll get there soon enough."

Sometimes their feet knocked loose small stones, which went rolling down the mountain behind them. Nando could hear the echoes of the stones tumbling farther and farther away, crashing against trees or bouncing off boulders.

"Don't look down," Manuel would remind him. "Just keep your eyes on the trail."

Up and up they climbed. They passed behind a thundering waterfall. They hiked through woods where the trees clung to the rocks. They scrambled over ridges and inched their way through openings between huge boulders.

"I call this place Fat Man Squeeze." Manuel laughed, and Nando laughed too.

Finally they reached a place where the path grew level. They walked a short way through a forest. Then at once they left the trees and stepped into a small green meadow, perched on top of a towering cliff. It seemed as though the whole world lay at their feet.

Far, far below, Nando could see the valley where he lived. The highway running up the valley, the one his school bus followed every day, looked like nothing more than a thin black ribbon. His school seemed no bigger than a matchbox. Across the tiny woods and fields he could see his town, with its little streets and stores and steeples. And beyond the town lay more mountains, peak after peak capped with snow.

"This is it—my secret lookout," Manuel said. "I'll show you why I call it Indian Cliff." He reached into the hollow of a tree. When he pulled his hand out, it held three small sharp stones.

"Arrowheads!" Nando cried.

"Yeah. I found them lying on the trail," Manuel said proudly. "I think the Indians used to camp here."

The boys walked close to the edge of the cliff—but not too close—and found two rocks for seats. Manuel took sandwiches and apples from his knapsack, and they had lunch while they shared the view.

They ate without saying much. They did not want to spoil the wonderful silence that comes from being so far above the rest of the world. Together they watched the shadows of the clouds drifting across the valley floor, and followed the hawks and eagles floating far below them. They sat gazing for half an hour. At last Manuel stood up to stretch his legs.

Then it happened, without warning! The rock Manuel was using for a seat suddenly shifted. It slid down the slope toward the brink of the cliff, carrying Manuel with it!

Manuel gave a yell and spread out his arms, trying to catch hold of something. He felt himself sliding over the edge, and then falling. His feet struck a ledge, and he stopped—but at once the ledge crumbled away, and he felt himself sliding down again. His fingers grabbed on to a jagged bit of rock, and with a jerk he came to a halt.

He looked straight down and saw his legs dangling over empty space.

He was hanging from the side of Indian Cliff.

He did not try to move. In a flash he knew where his only hope lay.

"Nando!" he screamed. "The rope! Tie it around the arrowhead tree, and lower it down to me!"

Somewhere above he could hear Nando scrambling along the top of the cliff and calling down to him. A little bit of earth, loosened from above in some way, struck him gently on the shoulders and neck. What if a large amount should come down before Nando could get the rope to him?

"But it won't—I'm sure it won't. Nando will send the rope down in a minute—and then I'll get out of this mess," Manuel told himself. But then he had a horrible thought: *"What if the rope is not long enough to reach me?"*

Manuel's fingers ached. With each passing second, it grew harder and harder to hold on. He knew that any movement might cause him to lose his grip. But slowly, slowly he turned his head, and strained his eyes to look up. And far above, he caught sight of the end of the rope. Nando was lowering it down the cliff!

Manuel watched it come slowly down the rock face, twisting and turning like a long, thin snake. Moving slowly, sliding, catching on bits of rock and then dropping again, the end came gradually nearer. And then it stopped—just a few inches above Manuel's hands!

"It's no good!" Manuel yelled. "I can't reach it!"

A second later the rope rose a short way back up the cliff. It hung there for a moment, its end waving and shaking in the air. Then it started down again—and this time it reached Manuel with two feet to spare.

Manuel held his breath, got a firm grip, and slowly began to pull himself up. He pulled with his arms, and pushed with his legs by sticking his feet into cracks in the cliff. Halfway up he had a terrible scare—the rope seemed to give a little, and at the same time he heard a cry from Nando somewhere above.

Now Manuel was only five feet from the top—now three feet—only one foot to go—now safety! With a shout of joy he pulled himself onto the top of the cliff.

spiny sea horse

What Type of Body Covering Do Fish Have?

Most fish have skin covered

with scales. Some scales are smooth.

Other scales are rough. Fish have gills,

fins, and a tail.

gill

scales

tail

fins

perch

How Do Fish Eat?

Most fish eat smaller fish, insects,

crabs, and other animals.

They catch food with their mouths.

Some fish eat plants.

false kelpfish

Where Do Fish Live?

Fish live in lakes, oceans, rivers, and other bodies of water.

Some fish live in freshwater.

Some fish live in salt water.

porkfish (with black stripes)
and grunts

How Do Fish Have Young?

Most fish hatch from eggs.

But some sharks give birth

to live young. The shark babies

grow inside a mother's body

until they are born.

lemon shark baby
and mother